*For*
Connie and Christien,
Thomas and Dominic
and Mrs Murphy
*~R.T.*

This edition produced for
The Book People Ltd
Hall Wood Avenue, Haydock, St Helens WA11 9UL, by
LITTLE TIGER PRESS
1 The Coda Centre, 189 Munster Road, London SW6 6AW
First published in Great Britain 2001
Text and illustrations © 2001 Rory Tyger
Artwork arranged through Advocate
Rory Tyger have asserted their rights to be
identified as the author and illustrator of this work
under the Copyright, Designs and Patents Act, 1988.
Printed in Belgium
1 3 5 7 9 10 8 6 4 2

# newton

*by*

Rory Tyger

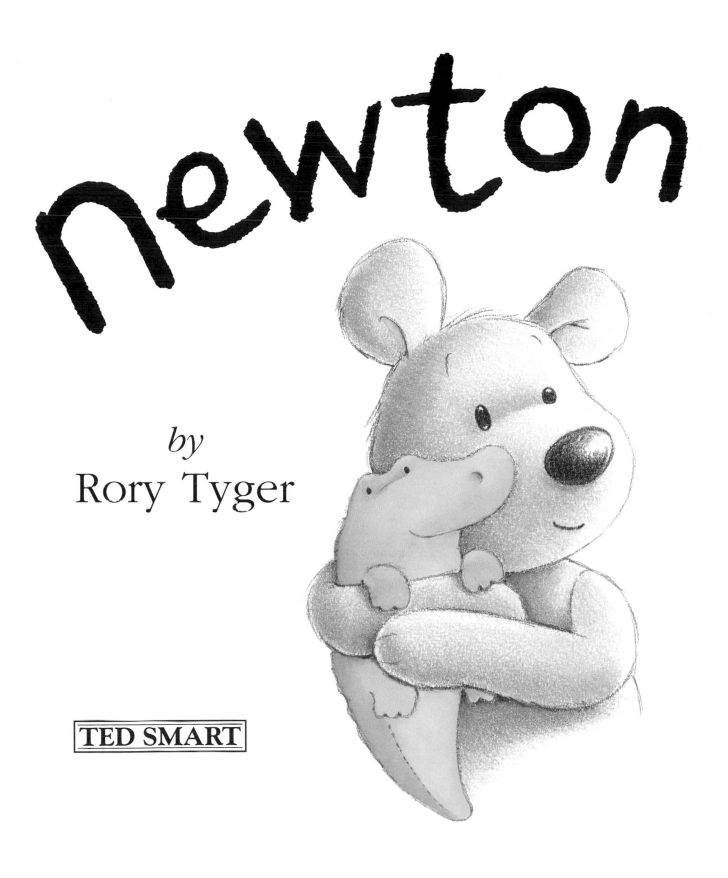

TED SMART

# CREAK, CREAK, CRE-E-EAK

Newton woke up suddenly.
There was a funny noise somewhere in the
room. "Don't be frightened," he told Woffle.
"There's always an explanation for everything."
He gave each of his toys a special cuddle
so they wouldn't be scared.

# CREAK, CREAK, CRE-E-EAK

went the noise again.

Newton got out of bed and turned on the light.
He walked across the room . . .

"See, toys," he said. "There's nothing to be frightened of. It's only the wardrobe door!"

Newton went back to bed again.

# FLAP! FLAP! FLAP!
What was that? Was it a ghost?

Once more Newton got out of bed. He wasn't really scared, but he took his bravest toy, Snappy, just in case. He tiptoed, very quietly, towards the noise.

FLAP! FLAP! FLAP!

it went again. "Of course!" said Newton . . .

"Just what I thought."
It was his bedroom curtains,
flapping in the breeze.
"I'll soon sort those out,"
said Newton.

"You were very brave,
Snappy," he said, as
he closed the window.

SPLISH!

SPLASH!

SPLISH!

Another noise!

Newton looked outside. It wasn't raining.
Besides, the noise wasn't coming from
outside.

Nor was it coming from
his bedroom. What was it?
"Stay right there, you two,"
said Newton, "while I look
around."

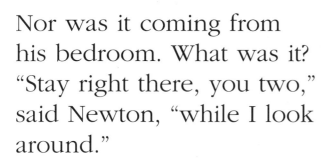

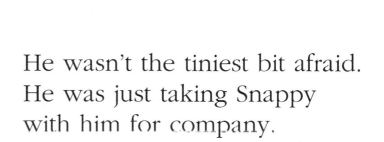

He wasn't the tiniest bit afraid.
He was just taking Snappy
with him for company.

Newton crept down the corridor. It was
very spooky, especially in the dark corners.

# SPLISH! SPLASH! SPLISH!

went the noise.

Very, very quietly, Newton
opened the bathroom door . . .

"Of course, we knew it was the bathroom
tap, didn't we, Snappy," said Newton.

Newton turned off the tap, and
tiptoed back down the corridor.
"Shh," he said to Snappy, just
in case *something* in the dark
corners sprang out at them.

Before he got into bed,
Newton pulled back the
curtains - just to check. It
was very, very quiet outside.
"No more funny noises,"
said Newton.

"You can go to sleep
now," he told all his toys.

# RUMBLE! RUMBLE! RUMBLE!

"Oh no!" cried Newton. "What's that?"

Newton listened very hard. Not a sound. He was just beginning to think he hadn't heard anything at all when

# RUMBLE! RUMBLE! RUMBLE!

There it was again!

Newton peered under his bed.
Nothing there at all - except for an
old sweet he'd forgotten about.
"Don't worry," said Newton. "We'll
soon find out what it is."

## RUMBLE!
Newton stood
very still.

## RUMBLE!
Newton listened
very hard.

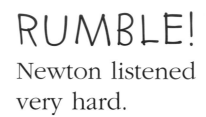

## RUMBLE! went the noise.
And suddenly Newton knew
exactly what it was!

Newton padded downstairs, and into the kitchen. He helped himself to a large glass of milk and two thick slices of bread and honey. And now he could hear no

RUMBLE! RUMBLE! RUMBLE!

at all, because . . .

the rumbling had been
his empty tummy!

Newton went upstairs again, and told his toys
about his rumbling tummy.
"There's always an explanation for everything,"
said Newton, as he climbed back into bed.
"Goodnight, everyone . . .

Sleep tight!"

SNORE, SNORE, SNORE,

went Newton.